SARAH LEAN grew up in Wells, Somerset, but
now lives in Dorset with her husband, son and
dog. She has worked as a page-planner for a
newspaper, a stencil-maker and a gardener,
amongst various other things. She gained a
first-class English degree and became a primary
school teacher before returning to complete an
MA in Creative and Critical Writing with
The University of Winchester.

*Jack Pepper* is Sarah's fourth story for children.

# Jack Pepper

## SARAH LEAN

### Illustrated by Gary Blythe

HarperCollins *Children's Books*

First published in Great Britain by HarperCollins *Children's Books* in 2014
HarperCollins *Children's Books* is a division of HarperCollins*Publishers* Ltd,
77-85 Fulham Palace Road, Hammersmith, London, W6 8JB.

The HarperCollins website address is: www.harpercollins.co.uk

1

Copyright © Sarah Lean 2014
Illustrations © Gary Blythe 2014

ISBN 978-0-00-755181-1

Sarah Lean asserts the moral right to be identified as
the author of the work.
Gary Blythe asserts the moral right to be identified as
the illustrator of the work.

Printed and bound in England by Clays Ltd, St Ives plc

**MIX**
Paper from
responsible sources
**FSC** www.fsc.org **FSC**™ **C007454**

# 1.

# Now

"Stop the car, Dad!" Ruby said. "Look, Sid, look at the lamp post."

Sid pressed his nose to the back-seat window.

"What is it this time?" Ruby's dad

said, enjoying trying to guess what Ruby might come up with next. "A ghost? A flying cat?" They'd had a long drive home after a day out at the Flight Museum, which meant Ruby's imagination was in full swing, keeping them all entertained.

"No, not this time! Now you've gone past it. Please stop, Dad!" Ruby said. "No, look, another one! Dad, stop there, under the next street light."

The urgency in Ruby's voice made

her dad steer the car towards the kerb. Ruby unclicked her seat belt and jumped out of the car.

"Where are you going?" her dad called. He turned round as he heard Sid's seat belt clunk and the back door open too.

Sid joined Ruby under the copper beam of the street light. Ruby was mesmerised by a poster stuck to it, a hand-drawn picture of a small white and ginger dog. It said: *Please help us find Jack Pepper.*

PLease help us find
Jack Pepper

"It is him, isn't it?" Ruby said.

"You wouldn't forget that dog," said Sid.

Ruby took in every last detail of the drawing. It couldn't be a coincidence. There couldn't be two dogs like this, two dogs called Jack Pepper.

# 2.

## THREE YEARS EARLIER

THE WORLD WAS UPSIDE DOWN AS RUBY slipped through the sky, lying back on the swing, looking at nothing but blue. She kicked against the invisible air. The weight of her body rocked from her head to her feet. The swing chain creaked; the fixing clicked.

Creaked. Clicked.

Creaked, like an aching heart.

"Thought you'd be here," a voice said.

Ruby sat upright, dizzy. She scuffed her toes through the sand to stop the swing.

"What are you doing?" It was Sid.

"Nothing, just swinging."

Sid punched his football at the ground and caught it. Bounced it again.

He saw the park was empty, and Ruby looked sad, which wasn't like her at all.

"Are you playing something by yourself?"

Ruby spun herself in the swing until the chain was taut, but it unfurled again as if it couldn't stand to be twisted. "I've got things I'm trying not to think about because it's too hard to think about them," she said. "It's easier on my own."

"We are on our own." Sid grinned, but there was barely a flicker of a smile from Ruby.

Ruby sighed. "My brother," she said. "Nothing's the same since he's been born and that's all I'm going to say about that right now."

"I won't say anything about that right now either," said Sid.

He glanced at Ruby to see if this was OK. Ruby caught his eye, blew out her cheeks, shrugged. The best agreement she could give.

"So I'll stay then," Sid said.

Ruby nodded. It was hard to be angry and sad, all mixed up. But Ruby knew if anyone could make her feel better Sid could. Sid wouldn't make things harder.

"Do you want to play football?" he said.

"Not really."

Sid dropped the ball, rolled it under his foot, thought hard, kicked it up and caught it.

"We could play your game?" he said.

"Which game?" Ruby said. Nothing was fun right now.

But Sid knew Ruby was the queen of disguising herself in her imagination.

"The adventure game, the one where we can be whoever we want to be," Sid said. "Then you won't have to think at all."

Ruby leaned her head back, squinted at the cloud above her collapsing and blooming from a ship with sails, to a giant face, into the shape of something yet to be. She allowed herself a smile.

Sid dropped his football again and pushed the swing to sway Ruby sideways.

"How do we start?" Sid said.

"There are no rules in this game, Sid. Start in the middle if you want."

He hauled one of the swing's chains and let it go again. Ruby swirled in an unpredictable arc.

Sid searched his mind for something that had nothing to do with Ruby's baby brother. They both stared at the cloud morphing. Saw the creature that roared to be set free.

"Dragon trainers," Sid said, rolling the magic words in his mouth. "The dragons are wild and fierce, but... well, they only like us and we've made them ours, but now we need to teach them things."

Ruby dragged her shoes through the sand. She liked the sound, soft and gravelly. Like the slow, lingering breath of a dragon. She pulled her feet back and heard scales shuffle, like scorched leaves, as the dragon emerged from her mind.

"Let's train them to fly," Ruby said, swinging again.

She kicked off from the ground,

shivering because of the huge dragon she imagined taking her up towards the clouds.

Sid jumped on the other swing. Ruby was already high, soaring on the magnificent creature. Free from the rules that tethered people to the ground.

"Do dragons have claws or paws?" Sid called from the other swing.

"There are no rules, Sid! It can have whatever you want!"

Ruby pushed harder, towards the deepest blue of the sky.

"I want claws for fighting!" Sid said.

They pitched and rocked.

Creak. Click. Creak. Click.

The seat of Ruby's swing lurched, as if it wanted to go further than the chains that anchored it to the frame. Ruby felt the weight of her body lift, as if she might keep going if she didn't hold on so tightly.

"And I want a whole heap of treasure," Sid called. "There's always treasure where there's dragons! And it's been stolen and we're going to get it back."

But for some reason the thought of treasure drew Ruby back to thinking about what had happened that morning.

Scales ruffled as Ruby imagined that her dragon dived towards the ground. Claws clattered, the dragon landed, lay down, coiled around the treasure.

The chain creaked.

The fixing clicked.

Ruby jumped from the swing.

# 3.

"I'M ALL RIGHT," RUBY SAID, BEFORE Sid could ask.

Sid dug his toes in to stop, leaped from his swing and ran over. Ruby rolled on to her back in the deep sand.

"Dragon stalled," she said.

She brushed the grains from her palms, wiped down her clothes and shook out her hair.

Sid collected his football. He watched Ruby as he punched his ball to the ground, bounce-bouncing it.

Ruby squinted, pointing at the cloud, liking the way her raised arm felt wobbly and giddy. Her smile faded as the dragon cloud bloomed, collapsed, dispersed and began to look like a baby in a cot, which reminded her of what had happened that morning.

"What would you do if you met a dragon?" Sid asked.

"Train it to fly, like we said."

"But that's in the game. I mean for real."

Ruby closed her eyes. Her imagination stretched, widened, began to eat her up. There was a dragon at home. A newborn dragon. Hatched, wrinkled, fierce and foul-smelling. Shrieking and demanding, cluttering up the arms of the mother dragon, making his sister feel left out. But she kept this to herself.

"It feels real," Ruby said, opening her eyes.

Sid squinted at her. Ruby was in her own world. He liked to go there with her though.

"You need to learn to balance,"

he said, "so when the dragon turns, you turn with it."

He helped her up off the ground and pulled her over to the see-saw. They climbed on, shuffled until the plank hovered, balanced in mid-air, their weight equal. Sid waited for Ruby to push the game further, like she usually did. But Ruby was quiet.

"If you really had a dragon, everyone would want to see it," Sid said.

Ruby pictured the dragon in a cage. She imagined everyone looking at it. In awe. In amazement. Their pride. Their joy. But how it roared and rattled the bars at her.

She wanted to say something to the baby dragon. But she couldn't find words it would understand. She didn't even know what those words were. She imagined the unspoken sounds in her chest, like dragon's breath. A swirling, hurtling ball of furious green flame. She let it out.

"Aaargh!" she yelled.

The searing sound hurtled across the park. It singed the football goalposts and stirred the trees over at the far side of the park, scorching everything the flames touched.

Sid clamped his hands over his ears. But the image of the baby dragon wouldn't leave Ruby. The creature ignored her yell and curled its retractable claws tighter. Ruby swung her leg over the see-saw handle, ready to jump again.

Sid let go of his ears to hold on to the see-saw because it tipped now that Ruby had moved. Ruby jumped. The end thumped down on the rubber tarmac and jolted Sid.

"Why were you shouting?" he asked.

"To see if the dragon could hear me."

Sid frowned, grabbed his ball and turned it in his hands.

"You sounded like a dragon," he muttered. "And stop jumping off things.

That hurt."

Ruby crouched beside the pillar at the middle of the see-saw and Sid sat beside her. She spat on her fingers and tried to wipe her hands clean. The dirt smeared. *I feel like a dragon in a cage,* Ruby thought.

Just then, a small white shape right in the middle of the football pitch caught Sid's eye.

Ruby pulled in her legs and rested her chin on her knees. She picked at the peeling rubber on the edge of her shoes.

She knew Sid was trying to cheer her up, but she couldn't seem to do anything right today. She felt heavy inside, and only pretending she was someone else, somewhere else, seemed to help her feel lighter.

"Sorry, Sid," she said. "I wish I knew how to stop feeling like this about my brother, but I don't know how."

"Let's keep playing the game," Sid said.

"I can't. Everything reminds me of what I'm trying not to think about."

Sid knew what the white thing in the middle of the pitch was now. A small dog, its ears turned towards them. The dog waited, watching them. Then a woman in a black skirt came into the park, tottering in high heels on the path alongside the pitch. She stopped when she noticed the little white dog. She looked all around. Walked on. Checked her watch. Turned back and looked again. Then she crossed the pitch, heading towards the dog, her hand held out.

Ruby was thinking about the tiny dragon at home, settled to sleep. How could it be so content when she was not!

"I can't even trust my imagination, Sid," Ruby whispered, as if the dragon shouldn't hear.

Sid remembered when he hadn't been picked for the football team and Ruby had invented a game of football in space against aliens. He was player of the match as she cheered from the sidelines.

"Yes you can, Ruby. Rules of the game," Sid said. "You're the best at this."

Ruby folded her arms, but her eyes twinkled. She knew Sid wasn't going to give up on her.

"I've told you before, there are no rules!" she smiled.

"Not even in space football."

Ruby remembered. She sighed. It was easier making someone else happy.

"Trying not to be jealous of my brother is really hard, Sid. And I don't think he likes me anyway."

"He's just a baby. They only know how to sleep and eat and poop."

"Thanks, Sid," Ruby muttered. "So you think he won't like me as soon as he learns how, because I'm not perfect like him."

"No, I didn't mean…"

"Anyway, I don't want to like him." Ruby caught her fingers in a tangle of her hair. She wasn't sure she meant to say that.

"You could pretend," Sid said. "You're good at pretending."

Ruby imagined being nice to the baby when anyone else was around.

But it was too hard. One minute she could choose whose lap to sit on, turn up her music if she wanted. Now she had to wait for her breakfast, nappies needed changing just when she had something important to say to her mum, and she had to be quiet most of the time because the baby was sleeping! The creature had invaded her life; it was ugly and unlovable. This didn't feel like a game at all.

"I don't think you're supposed to pretend to be nice," Ruby muttered.

Sid was still watching the woman get closer to the little dog. And an idea blossomed.

"But you said we can be whoever we want when we imagine it," he said. "Not what we do, but who we are, what we're like."

Ruby opened her mouth, but the words were unimportant. Sid understood something she hadn't. She was being the type of sister she didn't want to be.

"Even someone who isn't jealous of their brother."

Sid grinned. He held Ruby's hand and dragged her across the playing field. "In the meantime, one of our dragons has escaped!"

# 4.

"It's my game now," Sid said, as they ran towards the dog on the football pitch. "Just do as I say. Wave your arms and shout."

"Why?" Ruby asked.

"You'll see," he said.

Ruby's face lit up with the running and the warmth of the sun on her skin that made her cheeks glow. Her eyes sparkled and it felt as though this morning had never happened. Just for a minute she could be free to choose who she was.

The little white dog walked away from the woman who was still holding out her hand. His ears pricked and his tail swayed at the children racing towards him.

As he got closer, Sid saw it wasn't
a small dog, it was a puppy. Ruby saw it
then too. Small, white, with little sturdy
legs and circles like ginger biscuits on
his back. He had ginger fur like a mask
over his eyes, and ears that looked as if
he was hiding who he really was.

The woman was there already. She
bent down and picked up the puppy.
He paddled at the air, waiting for the
children to arrive. But he couldn't wait
any longer.

He wriggled free from the woman's

hands. He jumped, rolled and picked himself up and raced towards Ruby and Sid as if he knew just where he was going. Ruby saw him coming and, without thinking, bent and opened her arms and scooped him up.

"Oh, he's yours!" the woman said. "I thought he was lost."

Sid took a deep breath. "He belongs to Ruby." Ruby's eyes widened, a smile spread. "We thought we'd lost him for a minute," Sid said.

"Thank you for finding our escaped dragon. He's still in training," Ruby said, quick as anything. "But we haven't trained him properly yet."

The woman opened her mouth.

"Oh," Ruby said with a shake of her head. "You thought he was a puppy.

Well, it's a disguise." She put a finger to her lips and whispered, "You'll have to promise not to tell anyone or our people from the Society of Secret Dragon Trainers will probably find you and…" Ruby drew in her lips and shook her head slowly.

Sid mimed a slice across his throat and shook his head too.

The woman raised her eyebrows, smiled a little. "He should really be on a lead," she said.

"She only got him last week and he

hasn't got one yet," Sid said.

"We have to get back now, before he gets hungry," Ruby said. She swallowed. "You don't want to be near a dragon when it's hungry."

"Sweet little puppy," the woman said. "Very small for a dragon, but still, perhaps he should have a collar and a name tag?" She smiled. "What's his name?"

"Jack," Ruby said. The first word on her lips, the last words she meant to say. "Jack Pepper."

She froze for a moment then hugged the puppy in close. The real treasure. Jack Pepper. Her brother.

# 5.

THEY SAT IN THE GRASS AND THE PUPPY rolled over and bared his tummy. Ruby inspected the puppy's ears and eyes and fur for dragon scales and the seams that concealed him.

"That's where the zip would be for his disguise," she said. "Pull down the middle and out comes the dragon."

Sid held the delighted puppy's front paws.

"Claws, Ruby. For fighting battles. And look at his white teeth. One day they'll be strong and sharp, like swords."

Jack Pepper curled into the curve of Ruby's arm, rested his chin on her. He looked up with nothing but joy. Ruby marvelled. How had the puppy decided about her so quickly?

"He's gorgeous," she said, trying out the words. Surprised how easy it was to say, to feel. She'd heard someone say that just this morning. Not to her, of course.

The puppy's eyes closed. She thought of her baby brother at home. For some reason he was most unbearable to her while he was asleep.

Ruby plonked the puppy in Sid's lap and got up. The puppy woke, his tail curled under and he whistled softly at being disturbed.

"That's mean!" Sid snapped. He

pulled the tired puppy to his chest. "He's not your brother and he didn't do anything to you either."

Ruby's hair fell over her face; she rolled her ankles out and stared at the ground, feeling bad that being jealous made her unkind. She had peered through the crack of her baby brother's bedroom door that morning, heard the sound of his sleepy breath. She'd crawled into the warm milky smell of his room. She stared through the bars of the cot at the smooth face and tiny perfect hands, closed like new flowers. She reached out to stroke his cheek, but then he woke and suddenly started screaming and screaming and wouldn't stop. Mum and Dad rushed in, and they were cross and tired, and Ruby muttered under her breath that she wished the baby would just go away again.

"I don't want to keep the puppy," Ruby said.

"We're not going to." Sid sighed. "We need to find out where he came from. Please, let's just keep playing the game."

It hurt Ruby to think what she was thinking now. She was the one most wild and fierce, like an untrained dragon. But she was also the one who felt something valuable had been stolen from her.

"So now we have to take the dragon back to the training centre," Sid said. "Ruby!"

Ruby snapped out of her thoughts and nodded. *I can be whoever I want.* She held out her hands for the puppy. Sid wasn't sure.

"I will look after him," Ruby said.

"I know you will." Sid smiled and handed him over. "Now we need a clue," he said. "Like a big shed or something, where they keep the dragons."

Ruby carried the soft weight of Jack Pepper down the road next to the park, this time letting him sleep in her arms.

Sid knocked on a few doors, but there was nobody in. Then a little girl answered the door of number 52, blackcurrant juice curved in the corner of her mouth, her plaited hair unravelling.

"That's Mrs O'Donnell's puppy," she said. She leaned forward and pointed down the street. "The house behind the droopy tree, with all the bins out front. She's got a dog like that but bigger. She barks at the postman and she had five puppies." The girl smiled at Jack Pepper and stroked his ears. He woke. His tail bounced. "We were allowed to go and see them when they were born. Their eyes were closed and they squeaked when we picked them up."

"How small were they?" Ruby asked.

The little girl cupped her hands. "Like this."

"About the size of a big egg?" Ruby said, nodding as if she'd seen them herself. "They're not puppies. They're dragons in disguise."

The little girl tucked in her chin, twirled the end of her plait.

"Hatched from eggs," Ruby said.

"No they're not." The girl clasped her hands.

Ruby leaned in and whispered, "You know how you can tell?"

The little girl shook her head.

"Look in his eyes."

The little girl leaned closer to the puppy.

"There's no such thing as dragons," she whispered, as if she wasn't sure whether to tell Ruby this secret.

"Are you sure?" Ruby said.

"Ruby, let's go," Sid said. He thanked the little girl, who stared at Ruby now.

Ruby sighed, pulled Jack Pepper to her chest. They headed for the house with the willow tree and the bins outside.

Flip-flops smacked against the pavement, running after them.

"I want to look again," the little girl from number 52 said. She held the puppy's face. "It could be true," she murmured as she tried to look further.

Ruby grinned. "You see it now?"

The girl nodded.

"All dragons have treasure in their eyes," Ruby whispered.

"Like you do," the little girl said.

# 6.

Mrs O'Donnell's house looked like just the kind of place where newly-hatched precious dragons might live. Tall and wide with vines and ivy worming towards the windows. A double garage at the side. Some roof tiles missing. Ruby and Sid looked at each other.

"Do you think dragons live here?" Sid said.

"I think they grew too big for the garage," Ruby gulped.

The curled metal gates woven with chicken wire were ajar. That's how the puppy had escaped.

Knock knock.

Bark bark!

They listened. A door closed inside

the house. The children heard a woman's voice say, "All right, all right, Honey. I'll think of something to tell her."

Ruby stepped back. Did Mrs O'Donnell know she was here? And what was she going to tell her? Ruby looked at Sid. He shrugged. The door opened.

"Oh! Thank goodness, you found the puppy just in time!" Mrs O'Donnell said and her faded freckles smudged in her smile wrinkles.

"He was in the park," Ruby said. "The girl at number 52 said he was yours." She held Jack Pepper out, but not very far, suddenly unwilling to hand him over.

"I was expecting his new owner to arrive just now," Mrs O'Donnell said. She sunk her hand into the deep pocket of her long shirt and fed a treat to the puppy. "I thought you were her at the door, coming to collect him, and I wasn't sure what I was going to tell her!"

Ruby held the puppy tighter. Mrs

O'Donnell watched.

"He's quite special that dog, knows far too much for one so little and only nine weeks old," Mrs O'Donnell said. Ruby looked up at her. "But I think you might know that already."

Ruby wondered for a minute. She felt as if they'd come much further together than the short walk from the park.

Mrs O'Donnell turned her back, left the door wide. "Why don't you come in for a minute? I could do with a little help before his new owner gets here."

Ruby and Sid followed her in. Mrs O'Donnell waited for Sid to close the front door before she opened the second door inside.

"Honey!" she called. The ginger and white mother was already waiting, her nose twitching with familiar and new smells. She went straight to Ruby, stood on her hind legs against Ruby's legs. The puppy leaned down. They sniffed, wiggled and wagged. *But what had they said to each other?* Ruby thought.

Nothing and everything all at once, just like her mum did to her baby brother. Just like her mum did to Ruby sometimes, for no reason at all.

Honey jumped down and followed Ruby, still carrying the puppy, into the kitchen.

"He's the last one to go," Mrs O'Donnell said. "Come on then, let's see what we need to do."

Sid nudged Ruby. He was worried she hadn't handed the puppy over yet. Worried she may have imagined too much.

"It's a game, remember?" he whispered. "We can't keep him."

Ruby couldn't see the baby dragon any more. Only the treasure she held.

*I can be whoever I want to be.*

"I know," she whispered back. "I just want to hold him for a little bit longer."

"He needs a wash and a wipe," Mrs O'Donnell said. "And there's a blanket from their bed needs cutting up. They remember each other through their noses and it'll comfort the pup when he's in his new home."

Ruby pressed her nose to the top of the puppy's head and breathed in the warm puppy smell. She felt it in her heart too, kind of sweet and familiar.

Sid called Honey to him while Ruby took the scissors, sat on the kitchen floor and looked at the blanket, already with a cut edge. Mrs O'Donnell had cut some off and given a piece to each owner for the puppies as they left for their new homes. With Jack Pepper tucked in her lap, Ruby folded and cut the blanket until it was shared in two.

Mrs O'Donnell gave Ruby a flannel, warm with water.

"Wipe his eyes and ears, then his paws," she said.

"I think they're clean already," Ruby said. "I looked earlier."

"Wash him anyway," Mrs O'Donnell said. "Some dirt you can't see."

Ruby cleaned the invisible dirt.

Knock knock.

Bark bark!

"There now," Mrs O'Donnell said. "That'll be the lady I was expecting, his new owner."

She closed the kitchen door behind her. The front door opened. Voices. Sid crouched next to Ruby, nudged his shoulder into hers. The game had to end now.

"Dragon trainers was our best adventure," Ruby said, as the puppy washed her too.

Sid nodded. "And Jack Pepper's a special dragon," he said. "Well trained."

Ruby smiled. But that wasn't what she imagined.

"You know what, Sid? I think you're right about there always being treasure around dragons and I think it's easier to train a dragon if you're a bit like a dragon yourself. That way you know how to find the treasure."

Sid watched the smile fall from Ruby's face like a cloud shading the sun.

"I don't hate my brother," Ruby said. "I don't hate him at all."

Sid bit his lip. But he knew that already, because he knew Ruby.

"Babies and puppies can't do much

by themselves and they need their mums to help them with everything." She thought about the big sister she'd like to be, someone who protects and keeps the baby safe, like she had with the puppy. "I'm not jealous either," Ruby said. She thought of her brother in her mother's arms. "Well, maybe a bit."

Sid smiled. "I was four when my sister was born and I had to share lots of my toys and she was always crying. But after a while you get to teach them to do things, like play football." He grinned.

"She's actually quite good. And when someone was mean to her at school I said 'just tell me if they do it again' and that felt really good. But I think I should have much more pocket money than she gets. I am the eldest!"

Ruby held the puppy's face.

"Everyone says he's so… perfect," she said, thinking how scared she was that she wasn't like him.

Jack Pepper looked up at Ruby and she could tell he liked her just the way she was.

# 7.

THE KITCHEN DOOR OPENED.

"Hello," the young woman said. "I'm Lucy Allen." She held out her arms, but lowered them when Ruby didn't offer the puppy to her. "I hear you rescued my new puppy."

Ruby's eyes sparkled.

"From Cruella De Vil," Ruby said. Lucy and Mrs O'Donnell looked at each other. Sid blinked; Ruby nudged him. Another game! "She had about ten men with her, sticks and nets, and they meant business, didn't they, Sid?"

"She was going to turn him and loads of other puppies into a white coat with ginger spots," Sid said.

"And they didn't want witnesses. And they would have caught us. But he… he barked and growled and scared them off, and you might think he's small, but inside he's as big as a dragon."

Lucy tilted her head.

"Didn't I say when I first saw him, Mrs O'Donnell? There's something really special about that dog. Something in his eyes, something much bigger, hidden behind that mask."

"We saw it too," Sid said.

"And the little girl at number 52," Ruby said.

Lucy held out her hands again. Ruby

closed her eyes. Remembered her baby brother in his cot. So perfect he'd made her feel flawed.

Lucy stepped closer.

"We should go," Sid said to Ruby. She had to hand the puppy over now. "More dragons to train, Ruby," he whispered.

"I'm really grateful that you rescued him," Lucy said. "I can see he means a lot to you, even though you've only known him for just a short while. He means a lot to me too."

Ruby nodded.

"I know it sounds funny," Lucy said, "but when I first saw him, when he was even tinier and rounder than he is now, I looked into his eyes and I thought somehow I'll be all right with you around. And you know what? He makes me feel braver." She laughed. "Does that sound daft?"

Ruby held the puppy in front of her face. She shook her head as Jack Pepper looked back. It was real what Ruby felt right then. Like Lucy. That she was going to be all right with her new brother around. *I am who I want to be.*

"You'll need this blanket," Ruby said. "It's been shared out so all the puppies have a piece, so each one's got everything, all the warmth and softness and smells, to remind them of one another."

"Thank you," Lucy said.

"We gave him a name," Ruby said, handing him over. "Jack Pepper. But you don't have to keep it."

Lucy smiled. "I like that name a

lot." She kissed the puppy. "Hello, Jack Pepper," she said.

Like Ruby Pepper's little brother, Jack. Small and smooth and perfect.

"Why did you call him that name?" Lucy said.

"Oh, don't you know?" Ruby said. "He's a very famous dragon trainer."

# 8.

# Now

Ruby's eyes were wide as she looked at the poster of the dog, now three years older and grown. But the joy at seeing him again was soon squashed by the message – *Please help us find Jack Pepper*

– that he was lost.

Ruby's dad left the car engine running and got out to see what the children were staring at.

"Ruby, it's freezing out here. What's so imp—"

He saw the name on the poster, a name so familiar.

"We found this little dog at the park once, just after Jack was born," Ruby said.

"We rescued him," said Sid.

"He rescued me actually," Ruby said.

"He made me see I could be a good sister. I named him after Jack."

"Jack Pepper," her dad said, his voice full of pride for his precious girl as he realised the weight of what that had meant to Ruby. How hard it must have been for her to suddenly have a brother when she'd had her mum and dad all to herself for ten years.

Ruby was still mesmerised by the poster on the street light.

"That must be Lucy's phone number," she said. "Remember her, Sid?

She'll be lost without Jack Pepper. I know I would be."

Ruby looked back at the car. At her little brother, now three, strapped into his car seat, craning his neck to see out of the open door.

"Ruby!" Jack called. "I want to see too!"

Ruby went back to the car. She unclicked the belt, scooped her brother out and cradled him on her hip.

"Dad, I need to find out if Jack's OK. And Lucy."

Ruby's brother held her face and turned it towards him.

"I'm here," he said. "Look!"

Ruby kissed his pudgy hand. "There's another Jack Pepper. And he's just like you."

Ruby's dad had already tapped the phone number into his mobile and pressed call. He handed it to Ruby.

"Find out," he said and Ruby passed him Jack to hold.

But it wasn't Lucy who answered. It was a young boy called Leo.

"Hello?" Ruby said. "I'm phoning about the lost dog. I knew a little dog called Jack Pepper three years ago. His owner was called Lucy Allen."

Sid and Jack and Ruby's dad watched as Ruby listened to the voice on the end of the phone.

"It is him!" she mouthed.

They waited. The boy talked for ages as Ruby listened. She paced, looked at Sid. Her eyes wrinkled, her eyebrows drew together. Then she suddenly gasped, before saying goodbye.

"Well?" Sid and her dad said at once.

"Ruby!" Sid pressed. "What did they say?"

Ruby smiled at her brother. "Dragons always know how to find treasure."

"Tell us, for goodness' sake!" her dad

said. "Have they found Jack Pepper?"

Ruby opened her mouth, but her little brother was waiting for his turn to speak.

"I'm here!" he said. "Have I gone invisible?"

"They found him." Ruby smiled. "But you won't believe what happened to him this time..."

Find out what happened to
Jack Pepper in...

SARAH LEAN

Bestselling author of *A Dog Called Homeless*

Hero

A little dog
with the heart
of a lion

Turn the page to read an extract.

# 1.

I CAN FIT A WHOLE ROMAN AMPHITHEATRE in my imagination, and still have loads of room. It's big in there. Much bigger than you think. I can build a dream, a brilliant dream of anything, and be any hero I want…

*For most awesome heroic imagined gladiator battles ever, once again the school is proud to present the daydreaming trophy to… Leo Biggs!*

That's also imaginary. You have to pass your trumpet exam to get a certificate (like my big sister Kirsty), or be able to read really fast and remember tons of facts to get an A at school (like my best mate George), before anyone tells you that they're proud of you. Your family don't even get you a new bike for your birthday for being a daydreamer, even if you really wanted one.

Daydreaming is the only thing I'm

good at and, right here in Clarendon Road, I am a gladiator. The best kind of hero there is.

"Don't you need your helmet?" George called.

"Oh, yeah, I forgot," I said, cycling back on my old bike to collect it. "Now stand back so you're in the audience. Stamp your feet a bit and do the thumbs up thing at the end when I win."

George sat on Mrs Pardoe's wall, kicking against the bricks, reading his book on space.

"It says in here that meteors don't normally hit the earth," George said, "they break up in the atmosphere. So there aren't going to be any explosions or anything when it comes. Shame."

"Concentrate, George. You have to pretend you're in the amphitheatre, they didn't have books in Roman times... did they?"

"Uh, I don't think so. They might have had meteors though. People think you can wish on meteors, but it's not scientific or anything."

He didn't close the book and I could tell he was still concentrating on finding out more about the meteor that was on the news. So I put on my gladiator helmet (made out of cardboard, by me) and bowed to my imaginary audience. They rumbled and cheered.

"Jupiter's coming now. Salute, George, salute!"

*The king of all the Roman gods with arms of steel and a chest like hills, rolled into the night stars over Clarendon Road like a tsunami. Jupiter was huge and impressive. He sat at the back of the amphitheatre on his own kind of platform and throne, draped his arm over the statue of his lion and nodded. It was me he'd come to watch.*

I held up my imaginary sword.

"George!"

George punched the sky without looking up from his book. He couldn't see or hear what I could: the whole crowd cheering my name from the thick black dark above.

*Let the games begin!* Jupiter boomed.

*The gate opened.*

"Here he comes, George!"

"Get him, Leo, get him good."

*The gladiator of Rome came charging up the slope.* I twisted and turned on my bike, bumped down off the curb and picked up speed. *The crowd were on their feet already and I raised my sword…*

And then George's mum came round the corner.

"George! You're to come in now for your tea," she said.

I took off my helmet and put it inside my coat.

"In a minute!" George said. "I'm busy."

"It's freezing out here," she said.

I skidded over on my bike, I whispered, "George! Please stay! It is my birthday. You have to be here, I have to win something today."

"I'm fine," he called to his mum. "I've got a hat."

"Yes, but you're not wearing it." She came over, pressed her hand to George's forehead. "You've got homework and you're definitely running a temperature."

"Gladiators don't have homework," I said. George grinned.

"But George does," his mum said.

"Mum!" His shoulders sagged.

She shook her head. "I think you both ought to be inside. Come on, George, home now."

"Sorry, gotta go," he sighed. He slipped off the wall, pulled at the damp from the frosty wall on the back of his trousers. "I'll come and watch tomorrow."

"Do your coat up," George's mum said as they walked away.

George turned back. "Did you know that Jupiter is just about the closest it ever gets to earth right now?"

I looked up. Jupiter was here, in the night sky over Clarendon Road.

"Yeah, I know, George."

"I'll do some research for our Roman presentation."

"Yeah, good one, see you tomorrow."

"Leo!"

"What?"

He saluted.

I didn't want to go home yet though. I really wanted something to go right today.

I bumped the curb on my bike, cruised back into the arena.

*The gladiator of Rome was lurking in the shadows between the parked cars. I could smell his sweaty fighting smell, heard his raspy breath. Just in time I hoisted my sword over my head as he attacked. Steel clashed. I held his weight, heaved, turned, advanced, swung. We* smashed our swords together again. I felt his strength and mine.

The crowd were up: thousands of creatures and men stamped their feet in the amphitheatre of the sky. Their voices roared. Swords locked, I ducked, twisted, to spin his weapon from his hands. I didn't see the fallen metal dustbin on the pavement. I braked but my front wheel thumped into the side of it. I catapulted over the bin and landed on the pavement.

The crowd groaned. Jupiter held out

*his arm, his fist clenched. He punched his*
*thumb to the ground.*

I'd never thought that I could lose in my own imagination. Maybe I wasn't even that good at imagining. I lay there, closed my eyes, sighed. It warmed the inside of my cardboard helmet but nothing else. Everything was going wrong today.

I opened my eyes but it wasn't the gladiator of Rome looking down at me. It was a little white dog.

# 2.

I DIDN'T KNOW IF DOGS HAD IMAGINATIONS
or if they thought like us at all, but this
little dog looked me right in the eye
and turned his head to the side as if
he was asking the same question that I
was: How can you lose when you're the
hero of your own story? Which was a bit
strange seeing as nobody can see what's
in your imagination.

I leaned up on my elbows and stared back. The dog had ginger fur over his ears and eyes, like his own kind of helmet hiding who he really was, and circles like ginger biscuits on his white back.

"Did you see the size of that gladiator?" I said.

The little dog looked kind of interested, so I said, "Do you want to be a gladiator too?"

I think he would have said yes, but just then a great shadow loomed over us.

"Is that you dreaming again, Leo Biggs?" a voice growled.

It was old Grizzly Allen. He had one of those deep voices like it came from underground. If you try and talk as deep as him it hurts your throat.

Grizzly is our neighbour and the most loyal customer at my dad's cafe just around the corner on Great Western Road – Ben's Place. Grizzly was always in there. It was easier and a lot better than cooking for one, he said.

You might tell a dog what you're

imagining, or your best mate, but you don't tell everyone because it might make you sound stupid.

"I didn't see the bin. I couldn't stop."

Grizzly held out his hand and pulled me up like I was a flea, or something that weighed nothing.

"No bones broken, eh?" he beamed. "Perhaps just something bruised."

I checked over my bike. The chain had come off and the rusted back brake cable was frayed.

"Aw, man!" I sighed.

"Bit small for you now," Grizzly said. "Can't be easy to ride."

"Yeah, I know. I need a new one." I shrugged, but I didn't really want to talk about that. I'd had this bike for four years, got it on my seventh birthday; the handlebars had worn in my grip. They were smooth now, like the tyres and the brake pads and the saddle. I didn't want to say anything about how I'd thought my parents were getting me a new one for my birthday, today. I guessed they didn't think I deserved it yet. It wasn't like I'd passed my Grade 6 trumpet exam, like Kirsty had.

Grizzly picked up my bike as if it was as light as a can-opener, leaned it against his wall and lowered himself down, all six feet four of him folded into a crouch.

"Can't do anything with this here cable." He sort of growled in his throat, but I didn't know if that was because he couldn't fix it or because he was uncomfortable hunkered down like that.

The little dog watched Grizzly's hairy hands feeding the chain back on the cogs. Grizzly didn't have a dog and it looked odd, a great big man with that little white and ginger dog standing, all four legs square, by his side.

"Did you get a new dog, Grizzly?"

Actually there was nothing new about that dog, except he was new here in our road. I don't mean he looked old, because he didn't. He was almost buzzing with life. There was something ancient about him though. Like one of the gold Roman coins in our museum. Sort of shiny and fresh on the outside, but with years and years of history worn into them.

"He's not mine," Grizzly said. "This here is Jack Pepper." The little dog watched Grizzly's broad face and his tail swayed at the sound of his own name.

# YOUR CHANCE TO WIN...

# Do you have a pet that's a real life hero?

Tell us a special story about him or her and we'll enter you into our prize draw. The winner will get a brand new Kindle Fire HD. Plus, we'll sponsor a dog in your name with Dog's Trust, and – to remind you of your very own hero – we'll send you a gorgeous fluffy toy dog.

Visit
**www.sarahlean.co.uk/herocompetition**
for details.

Terms and Conditions apply. Closing date: 30th April 2014.

*My name is Cally Louise Fisher*
*and I haven't spoken for thirty-one days.*
*Talking doesn't always make things happen,*
*however much you want it to.*

Cally saw her mum, bright and real and alive.
But no one believes her, so Cally stopped talking.
Now a mysterious grey wolfhound has started
following her everywhere. Perhaps he knows that
Cally was telling the truth...

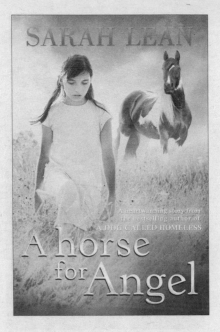

*Sometimes when things are broken*
*you can't fix them on your own –*
*no matter how hard you try.*

When Nell is sent to stay with distant family,
she packs a suitcase full of secrets. A chance
encounter with a wild horse draws Nell to Angel
– a mysterious, troubled girl who is hiding secrets
of her own. Both girls must learn to trust each
other, if they are to save a hundred horses…

Memories scoop you up and take you
back to another time, so you can feel things
all over again. I think of how important it is
for all of us, but especially for Grandad, to
remember the bright things from the past. But
now he's forgotten everything and he hasn't
told me his most important memory yet
– the one about a whale…

Can Hannah piece together the extraordinary story
that connects Grandad's childhood to her own?

# WORLD BOOK DAY fest

## Want to READ more?

**Visit** your LOCAL BOOKSHOP

- Get some great recommendations for what to read next

- Meet your favourite authors & illustrators at brilliant events

- Discover books you never even knew existed!

 **FIND YOUR LOCAL BOOKSHOP** WWW.BOOKSELLERS.ORG.UK/BOOKSHOPSEARCH

**Join** your LOCAL LIBRARY

You can browse and borrow from a HUGE selection of books and get recommendations of what to read next from expert librarians—all for FREE! You can also discover libraries' wonderful children's and family reading activities.

**FIND YOUR LOCAL LIBRARY** WWW.FINDALIBRARY.CO.UK

## GET ONLINE!

Visit **WWW.WORLDBOOKDAY.COM** to discover a whole *new* world of books!

- Downloads and activities
- Cool games, trailers and videos
- Author events in your area
- News, competitions and new books —all in a **FREE** monthly email

 AND MORE!

Don't forget to visit Sarah's website:

# www.sarahlean.co.uk

for news, competitions, downloadable wallpapers
and ecards you can send to your friends...

Plus information about all of Sarah's books